D1451372

Atheneum
Macmillan Publishing Company
866 Third Avenue
New York, NY 10022

Macmillan Publishing Company is part of the
Maxwell Communication Group of Companies.

First U. S. edition

Originally published by
Pan Macmillan Children's Books, London

Printed in Hong Kong

10 9 8 7 6 5 4 3 2 1

Library of Congress Catalog Card Number: 93 74731

ISBN 0 689 31898 7

GRAHAM OAKLEY

The Foxbury Force

PC Sweet   PC Plumb   PC Bouncer   PC Towsle   PC Cool
PC Farthing Sgt. Bumper Inspector Flannel PC Cosy   PC Preen

ATHENEUM 1994 NEW YORK

Maxwell Macmillan International
NEW YORK OXFORD SINGAPORE SYDNEY

Every morning at eight o'clock sharp, rain or shine, all the
constables of the Foxbury Constabulary paraded in front of the

Foxbury police station to be inspected by Sergeant Bumper and
Inspector Flannel.

On the second
Thursday of each month,
while the inspection was
going on, the Town Burglars
would get busy. Their job was to
"burgle" one shop per month and
then try to escape with the loot so that
the constables could get in some practice
at chasing burglars.

They were usually caught by teatime. If they weren't, they had to give themselves up because Foxbury Town Council wasn't all that keen on paying overtime.

But on one particular Thursday things were going to be different. The Foreman Burglar, who had a bad side to his character, had made a plan. "This time, when we burgle the jewellers we'll *really* escape and keep all the stuff ourselves and we'll be very rich."

He hadn't told the others about his plan because he knew they were too honest to be trusted. When they passed the police station, the Town Burglars created a terrific hullabaloo, just as they always did, to let the constables know that they'd done a burglary and were ready for the chase. The Foreman Burglar tried to keep them quiet, but he was just wasting his breath.

Inspector Flannel
was a jolly good sport
and he always liked to give
the Town Burglars a head start.
So today, like every other time, he
counted up to twenty very slowly.
Then he shouted, "Constables,
on your marks . . .
Get set . . . Go!"
And the chase
was on.

But it wasn't at all like one of their usual car chases.

Teatime went by, and even suppertime, but nothing the Town

He just drove on and on until at last . . .

There was no coffee break or lunch break or mid-afternoon snack.

Burglars could say or do would make the Foreman Burglar stop.

. . . he arrived at the old castle, just as he'd planned it.

"Escaping is against the rules. Give yourself up this instant!" shouted Inspector Flannel at the Foreman Burglar.

"Go and jump in the lake!" shouted the Foreman Burglar at Inspector Flannel.

"A situation like this calls for decisive action," said Inspector Flannel. "What we'll do is we'll . . . ummm . . . err . . . ahhh . . . we'll . . . err . . ."

"We could make a rope by tying our clothes together and climb up the castle wall," suggested PC Cosy.

" . . . make a rope by tying our clothes together and climb up the castle wall," continued Inspector Flannel.

When the rope was ready
PC Bouncer, who was very
strong, threw one end of it
up on to the battlements.

Then they all swam across
the moat and climbed up to
the castle roof.

Below them they saw the Town Burglars. They really looked as
if they'd started to enjoy being proper burglars.

"We'll rush straight down there and take them all by surprise," said Inspector Flannel. "Follow me, and keep close together."

But they didn't rush "straight" anywhere because they'd forgotten to bring a torch, and Inspector Flannel couldn't see very well in the dark.

It took them at least half an hour to find the door of the banqueting hall. They made so much noise doing it that the Town Burglars knew they were coming before they were half way there and had bags of time to get ready for them.

So when the Foxbury Constabulary at last launched their surprise attack

the only people who were surprised were the Foxbury Constabulary.

But the situation wasn't as bad as it looked. The armour had stood in the damp old hall for centuries, and it had got very rusty and stiff in the joints. Once they'd put it on, the Town Burglars found that they could hardly move at all. That was a great relief to the constables. Instead of the pitched battle they had been dreading they just had to carry out a simple mopping-up operation.

Next morning, the Town Burglars were loaded on to the truck and, while that was being done, PC Farthing tried to untie the knots in the rope of uniforms. But they were much too tight to be undone.

"Never mind," said Inspector Flannel, "we'll just have to go as we are. We're quite decent." Then he ordered the drawbridge to be lowered, and down it came with a terrific crash.

It was a pity that nobody had remembered to move the
police car first. Still, they all managed to pile into the Town
Burglars' truck.

They were nearly home when they came to a steep hill, and the
truck could only climb it very, very slowly. The constables were
playing "I spy with my little eye", and it was PC Sweet's turn to
spy something. "I spy with my little eye something beginning
with . . . umm . . . B," she said.

It was really surprising how everybody got the answer at
exactly the same time. "BANDITS!" they all cried.

As it was a Foxbury Council truck the only loot the bandits
were hoping for was perhaps a second-hand pick or shovel.

So when they saw the pile of silver
and jewellery they couldn't believe their
luck. Without stopping to think they rushed
around the back of the truck and dropped the rear
flap. *That* was a mistake. After the bandits had been
rounded up the constables went to the bottom of the
hill and let the burglars out of their armour. They were
pretty bilious and giddy at first, but when they were
feeling better they gave a hand to pick up the jewels and
silver. Then they all set off on the last few miles to Foxbury.

It was marketday when they arrived, and the streets were very crowded. So Inspector Flannel decided to have a Triumphal Procession into town just to show everybody what a wonderful police force they had. And as the Town Burglars had more or less redeemed themselves by foiling the bandits, he let them join in the procession and share the glory.

There wasn't much glory for the bandits, though. In fact, you could say they had a pretty rotten day. But in the end things didn't turn out too badly for them because they all sold their life stories to the newspapers and became rich and famous.

THE END